ST REGINA'S
CLASS

Mrs Bottomley-Blunt

Headmistress.
Has a long, laminated List of Rules.
Makes a noise like a horse when she is annoyed, which is a lot.

Mr Nidgett

Teacher of 4B.
Firm believer that everything can be mended with kindness.
Often proved wrong.

Stanley Bradshaw

Fond of footling, fiddle-faddling and shilly-shallying, much to Mrs Bottomley-Blunt's annoyance.

Manjit Morris

Stanley's best friend.
Determined to be the First Human Boy ever to do a lot of dangerous, foolish and impossible things.

Keith Mears

Self-proclaimed King of the Internet.
Falls asleep in class a lot.

PRIMARY

4B

Lionel Dawes

Called Lionel, even though she is a girl, because her mum says names do not have genders, they are just words, which is true if you think about it, but Mrs Bottomley-Blunt does not agree.

Bruce Bingley

Once got a plastic brontosaurus stuck up his nose for a week. Can burp the national anthem.

Lacey Braithwaite

Compulsive liar.

Penelope Potts

Annoying telltale. Identical twin of Hermione Potts in 4A, and determined to join her by fair means or foul.

Muriel Lemon

Knows too many medical facts. Fond of warning Mr Nidgett of the dangers of everything.

Harvey Barlow

Eater of many biscuits. Often mistaken for a Year 6.

Joanna Nadin

THE
WORST
CLASS
IN THE
WORLD
Gets Worse

Illustrated by
Rikin
Parekh

BLOOMSBURY
CHILDREN'S BOOKS
LONDON OXFORD NEW YORK NEW DELHI SYDNEY

BLOOMSBURY CHILDREN'S BOOKS
Bloomsbury Publishing Plc
50 Bedford Square, London WC1B 3DP, UK

BLOOMSBURY, BLOOMSBURY CHILDREN'S BOOKS and the Diana logo
are trademarks of Bloomsbury Publishing Plc

First published in Great Britain in 2021 by Bloomsbury Publishing Plc

A catalogue record for this book is available from the British Library

ISBN: PB: 978-1-5266-1188-8; eBook: 978-1-5266-1186-4

2 4 6 8 10 9 7 5 3 1

Printed and bound in Great Britain by CPI Group (UK) Ltd, Croydon CR0 4YY

For Jude and Siân
and all the other long-suffering Mr Nidgetts
who are doing an extraordinary job
teaching small people

– J.N.

For Ernest Ayeh–Datey,
Mr Nidgett incarnate

– R.P.

Our class is the **WORST CLASS IN THE WORLD**.

I know it is the **WORST CLASS IN THE WORLD** because Mrs Bottomley-Blunt (who is our headmistress, and who makes a noise like a horse when she is annoyed, which is a lot) is always taking our teacher into the corridor and saying,

'Mr Nidgett, I have come across some rotten eggs in my time, but 4B is **LITERALLY** the **WORST CLASS IN THE WORLD**.'

LITERALLY means actually scientifically **TRUE**. Mrs Bottomley-Blunt pointed that out when Manjit Morris (who is my best friend, and who is going to be the First Human Boy to Walk a Tightrope in Space) said his head had **LITERALLY** exploded when he got a dog called Killer for his birthday, and it actually hadn't.

It is true that a lot of things do not go as well as they could in class 4B. For example:

1. The time we had a battle to be the Biscuit King of 4B and Harvey Barlow was sick on Mr Nidgett's shoes.

2. The time Lionel Dawes got nits and gave them to everyone else including Mrs Bottomley-Blunt because her mum does not believe in CHEMICALS or killing anything with a face.

3. The time we went on a school trip to Grimley Zoo and Harvey Barlow smuggled a penguin back on the bus.

Plus no one has won a prize all year, and 4A have won:

1. Best Show and Tell
2. Best Lining Up in the Playground without Fighting
3. Best Cardboard Sarcophagus

Although this is not surprising, as their class captain is Eustace Troy, who is president of chess club, first violin in the school orchestra and team leader on the Shining Examples competitive spelling squad.

Our class captain is Bruce Bingley, who can only burp the national anthem, which I think is quite impressive, but Mrs Bottomley-Blunt does not.

BURP!!

She says school is not about footling or fiddle-faddling or **FUN**. It is about **LEARNING** and it is high time we tried harder to **EXCEL** at it.

Dad says well at least I haven't been arrested. Grandpa says being arrested would be getting off lightly and **IN HIS DAY** he had to walk five miles to school barefoot and eat gravel for lunch.

Mum, who works at the council, says, 'I have spent all day listening to Mr Butterworth bang on about bollards and the last thing I need is a heated debate about eating gravel. As long as Stanley's happy, that's all that matters.'

And you know what? I am happy, because:

1. According to Mr Nidgett, everyone excels at something, even Harvey Barlow – they just have to look very hard to find it.

2. According to the laws of probability, we have had all our bad luck and nothing else can possibly go wrong.

3. According to Manjit, even if it does

go wrong we have a FOOLPROOF PLAN to get away with it, which is DO NOT TELL ANYONE.

You see, 4B may be the **WORST CLASS IN THE WORLD**. But I like it.

The Playground Monitor

Lacey Braithwaite says it's
Penelope Potts's fault for being too
strict as a playground monitor.

Penelope Potts says it's Manjit
Morris's fault for telling us to hide
in the toilets instead of monitoring

out on the playground.

Manjit Morris says it's Lionel Dawes's fault for saying his War of the Wizards wand was biodegradable and could be flushed down the toilet.

Mr Nidgett says he doesn't actually care whose fault it is as long as the Playground Monitor Madness is finished or he will **LITERALLY** resign from teaching and become a daredevil stuntman because it cannot be harder than this.

But if you think about it, it's actually Mrs Bottomley-Blunt's fault, because she's the one who said we could be playground monitors in the first place.

What happened was we were in assembly, which usually goes like this:

1. Major Wellington, who is deputy head, and also in charge of Class 4A, reminds us about UNIFORM RULES and about being NEAT and OBEDIENT at all times, especially in assembly.

2. Mrs Bottomley-Blunt, who is our headmistress and who makes a noise like a horse when she's annoyed, which is a lot, hands out several Golden Stars to Eustace Troy, who is in 4A.

3. Hermione Potts, who is also in 4A, and who is vice president of chess club, chemistry club and astronomy club, and second best on the Shining Examples competitive spelling squad, plays 'All Things Bright and Beautiful' on her violin and gets another Golden Star.

4. Everyone sings 'Morning Has Broken', except for Bruce Bingley, who burps it instead, and gets a Golden Star taken away.

5. Everyone troops back to class, and 4B goes last, because of not being NEAT and OBEDIENT, except for Penelope Potts, who is the twin of Hermione Potts, who says it's not fair and she should be allowed to troop back with 4A and stay there forever because she has been NEAT and OBEDIENT for a MILLION MINUTES, only Major Wellington

does not agree and nor does Mrs Bottomley-Blunt.

Only in this assembly there was a **SURPRISE**, because after Mrs Bottomley-Blunt had deducted a Golden Star from Bruce Bingley for burping 'If I Had a Hammer', instead of saying, 'Classes dismissed, except you, 4B, you can all wait until the end,' she said, 'Now everyone sit **STILL** and **LISTEN** because I have an **IMPORTANT ANNOUNCEMENT**. That means even you, Mr Mears!'

Mr Mears is actually Keith Mears, who wasn't not listening but was actually asleep as usual, which he claims is because he has been doing so much homework, but is actually because he is in a long-running game of War of the Wizards against Mingyu Kim, who is the Korean champion and also in a different time zone. And so Bruce Bingley poked Keith with the plastic brontosaurus that was once stuck up his nose for a week and got another Golden Star

deducted, which he pointed out
was unfair because actually he
was being **NEAT** and **OBEDIENT**
and **HELPFUL**, but Mrs Bottomley-
Blunt didn't agree.

Then **FINALLY** Mrs Bottomley-
Blunt told us the **IMPORTANT**

ANNOUNCEMENT, which was that it was 4B's turn to be playground monitors next week and perhaps it would teach us something about **DISCIPLINE** and also being **NEAT** and **OBEDIENT**.

So then we were all **MAD** with excitement because whoever is playground monitor gets a bell to ring for beginning and end of break and a whistle to blow if they spot any **HOO-HA**.

And they get a red pen and notebook to write down the **HOO-HA** and report it back to Mrs Bottomley-Blunt after break.

Mostly the reports are about us, e.g.:

1. The time Lionel Dawes (who is called Lionel even though she is a girl because her mum says names do not have genders, they are just words, which is true if you think about it) started a sit-in protest to stop our caretaker (who is called Mr Spigot and has one ear bigger

than the other) mowing the grass,
because grass is a living thing and
has FEELINGS.

2. The time Bruce Bingley ate a fly
for a dare and then claimed he had
gained special Fly Superpowers and
would be sick on anyone who crossed
him and the sick would be Supersick
and would melt them into infinity.

3. The time Manjit started a craze for
playground swaps and Keith Mears
tried to swap his little brother Kevin
for a packet of crisps, but that's
another story.

We were all arguing over who would get to ring the bell first and blow the whistle first and hold the red pen and notebook first when Mrs Bottomley-Blunt made a noise like a horse and shouted, 'Being a playground monitor is a big **RESPONSIBILITY** and also **HARD WORK** and if you are not up to the task then no one will get the bell or the whistle or the red pen and notebook and 4A will be monitors again because they can be trusted not to cause **MAYHEM**. Now **ARE YOU UP TO THE TASK?**'

And we all nodded because we were
DEFINITELY up to the task and she
said in that case Mr Nidgett could
appoint the monitors and assembly
was over.

Then everyone trooped back to class, and 4B went last, because of not being **NEAT** and **OBEDIENT**, except for Penelope Potts, who said it wasn't fair and she should be allowed to troop back with 4A and stay there forever because she had been **NEAT** and **OBEDIENT** for a **MILLION MINUTES**. But Mr Nidgett reminded her that if she was in 4A she wouldn't be playground monitor.

So she said, 'Does that mean I'm first playground monitor then?'

And Mr Nidgett said actually he
was going to put all our names into
a hat (which is his actual hat and
is red and woolly) and pick pairs
for each day, because that was the
only fair way.

Except Penelope Potts said it
was not.

And Manjit said, 'Is.'

And Penelope said, 'Is not.'

And Manjit said, 'Is.'

And then Mr Nidgett said
actually he had already picked
the first pair while they were

busy arguing and in fact it was
Harvey Barlow and Penelope Potts,
and Penelope said that actually
it was very fair after all and she
would be the **BEST PLAYGROUND
MONITOR EVER** and then Mrs
Bottomley-Blunt would probably
put her in 4A after all.

 And Manjit said, 'Will not.'

And Penelope said, 'Will.'

And Manjit said, 'Will not.'

And Mr Nidgett said to please

stop arguing or we would prove

Mrs Bottomley-Blunt right that

we are **NOT** up to the task and perhaps we could get on with writing about how important bees are and why, which we did.

But then we were all arguing about why bees were so important, e.g.:

1. Lionel said it was because of POLLEN.

2. Harvey said it was because of HONEY.

3. Keith said it was because of STINGS.

Which is when Muriel Lemon
said stings were actually mortally
dangerous, i.e. if you got one you
might **DIE**, so in fact all bees were
KILLER BEES if you thought about
it, which we did, and agreed was
true.

Only then
Bruce said in
fact he had
been stung
by a **KILLER
BEE** and
survived.

Keith said in fact he had been stung by **TEN** killer bees and survived.

Manjit said he was going to be the First Human Boy to **LICK TEN MILLION KILLER BEES** and survive.

But that was when Mr Nidgett said he had picked the rest of the playground monitors out of the hat and if we could stop arguing long enough he would tell us who they were, so we did, and two of them were me and Manjit and we were **MAD** with excitement for the rest of the day so we didn't even care that we had the whistle blown at us four times for breaking rules in the playground, because next week we would be the ones with the whistle and it would be **ALL CHANGE**.

Mr Nidgett said, let's hope so. And also to please not lick any bees.

So all Friday and all weekend me and Manjit did not lick even one bee because we were too **MAD** with excitement about being the **MANLEY** Monitors, which is our brand name, and is half Manjit, half Stanley, and we would have a **FOOLPROOF PLAN** to be the **BEST PLAYGROUND MONITORS EVER** and probably get a medal.

And the next week on Monday
we were even **MADDER** with
excitement because when we got
into class the bell and the whistle
and the red pen and notebook
were already there, sitting on Mr
Nidgett's desk, and everyone went
'Oooooh' and 'Aaaaah' but then
started arguing about how many
dongs of the bell were the law
until Penelope Potts said actually
it was three dongs and she would
be doing them because she was
in charge of dongs and whistles

And that is when Mr Nidgett
said if he had to listen to any
more did/did not arguments then
no one would be playground
monitor at all, he would just do
it himself, and did we want that?

And everyone agreed that we
definitely did not want that and so
we did not argue once. Mr Nidgett

said he was very impressed, and that perhaps at break it would be our **TIME TO SHINE**, because he says we all have a **TIME TO SHINE**, it's just that ours has been a long time coming.

But it did not come today either because at break Penelope reported us for a lot of things, e.g.:

1. Bruce for claiming he was actually royal.

2. Keith for claiming he was actually dead.

3. Manjit for claiming Major Wellington is actually a vampire, and would LITERALLY kill Penelope if she didn't stop reporting us.

4. All of the rest of us for trying to tunnel to Finland.

Mr Nidgett said all in all it was very disappointing, but perhaps tomorrow would be a better day. Manjit said it would definitely be a better day because Muriel Lemon (whose parents are both doctors, and who is excused from all dangerous activities, e.g. netball, football and science experiments) and Lionel Dawes would be in charge of the bell and the whistle and the red pen and notebook, and they were more sensible.

But on Tuesday Lionel and Muriel were not more sensible. They reported:

1. Harvey Barlow for accidentally dropping his crisps, because that was littering, which is against the planet.

2. Bruce Bingley for trying to shoo a pigeon away from the crisps, because that was prejudiced against living things.

3. Harvey Barlow for following the pigeon into the Smelly Death Log (i.e. the hollow log with the bird poo on it, which no one even goes

near unless they are up to NO GOOD.
Not since Bruce Bingley claimed it
had an ancient curse on it and if you
touched the poo for more than a
second you would be swallowed by
the Ghost Pigeon).

4. Manjit for saying the pigeon WAS the Ghost Pigeon and he would VANQUISH it with his War of the Wizards wand, because that was against the planet AND prejudiced against living things.

Only Keith said the pigeon was
dead already so it wasn't against
anything living.

 And Lionel said, 'Is not.'

And Keith said, 'Is.'

And Lionel said, 'Is not.'

And Keith said, 'Is.'

And then we noticed Harvey
Barlow was stuck and had to
fetch Mr Spigot to pull him
out, which Mr Nidgett said was
very disappointing, and that we
definitely needed to do better
tomorrow, and that it was down

to me and Manjit to **RESCUE
THE SITUATION**. And Manjit
said we would, because we had
a **FOOLPROOF PLAN** to make it
happen.

So all the way home, me and Manjit
tried to think of that **FOOLPROOF
PLAN**.

Manjit said we could just report
4A for breaking rules. Only I said
that 4A didn't **EVER** break any
rules, which Manjit agreed was
true.

Then I said we could **MAKE** 4A
break some rules. Only Manjit said
that was against the rules, which I
agreed was true.

Manjit said, 'We are **LITERALLY**
going to be the **WORST MONITORS**
EVER and now I will never get a
job as a billionaire!' Which is his
number two ambition after being
the First Human Boy to do a lot of
things.

And I said, 'Unless we all stay
out of trouble.'

Manjit said that was impossible

unless we, e.g. stayed in the toilets all lunchtime and didn't even go near the playground. And I said we could definitely do that, and Manjit agreed, and so that was our **FOOLPROOF PLAN!**

When we got to school the next day, everyone agreed that it was almost definitely a **FOOLPROOF PLAN**, and so when it was breaktime, instead of going to the playground with the bell and the whistle and the red pen and notebook, we all trooped to the toilets.

Everything started well because, even though it was a **SQUASH** being in there, we all just stood by the sinks and discussed who would win in a fight, the

Ghost Pigeon or the Killer Bee
(and it was the Ghost Pigeon,
who is immune to stings), and
ate our snacks.

But that's when the **HOO-HA**
began. Because
Bruce Bingley
went to put his
banana skin in the bin, only
Lionel said it would be better to
FLUSH it down the toilet because
in fact it was biodegradable, i.e. it
would disappear into **NOTHING**.
So Bruce did.

So then Harvey Barlow went
to put his jam sandwich in the
bin, because he had dropped it
on the floor trying to show Keith
Mears how he could catch a
whole jam sandwich in his mouth
but he could not, so now it was
CONTAMINATED. Only Lionel said
it would be better to flush **THAT**
down the toilet too. So he did.

Then everyone started arguing
about what was flushable and
what was not. And Lionel said
she would decide and she said the

things that were flushable were:

    I. Lacey Braithwaite's stick of celery that might have been licked by a bee and was CONTAMINATED.

    2. Bruce Bingley's piece of cheesy biscuit that he had thrown at Penelope Potts and was CONTAMINATED.

    3. Penelope Potts's sock that had cheesy biscuit on it and was CONTAMINATED.

And the things that were not flushable were:

1. Muriel Lemon's shoe, that had trodden on the jam sandwich and was CONTAMINATED.

2. Manjit's War of the Wizards wand that had poked the shoe that had trodden on the jam sandwich and was now CONTAMINATED so it was unusable because its magic was GONE.

3. Harvey Barlow.

Only Manjit said in fact his War of the Wizards wand was actually biodegradable

because it was made of wood
and paint and they would both
definitely disappear into **NOTHING**
eventually and Lionel said she
would **PUT IT TO THE PEOPLE**,
which means have a vote, because
she is very keen on votes, and
the **PEOPLE** said it was definitely
biodegradable and Lionel agreed,
so Manjit flushed it.

But that is when it happened.

First the toilet water brimmed
up to the lid.

Then it brimmed over the edge.

Then it brimmed round all our shoes, which were all **CONTAMINATED**, but we could not flush them because they weren't biodegradable.

Then it brimmed out the door, which is when we went outside and realised everyone else had gone in and we hadn't even got to ring the bell for end of break **OR** use the whistle **OR** the red pen and notebook. Which is when Mr Nidgett arrived and saw the brimming and said, 'What in the name of Agamemnon have you done this time?'

So we told him and he said he didn't actually care whose fault it was as long as the Playground Monitor Madness was finished or he would **LITERALLY** resign from teaching and become a daredevil stuntman because it could not be harder than this, and also to quickly fetch Mr Spigot to mend the toilet and mop up before Mrs Bottomley-Blunt found out.

Only then a voice said, 'Find
out **WHAT**, Mr Nidgett?' and it
was Mrs Bottomley-Blunt, who

said, 'You are **LITERALLY** the
WORST CLASS IN THE WORLD!'

And she banned us from being playground monitors and put us on Tidying Paint Pot Duty instead and said if we didn't buck up our ideas we would be tidying paint pots **UNTIL KINGDOM COME**, and even though we do not know what Kingdom is, we know it has never come yet.

When I got home I told Mum and Dad and Grandpa about never being playground monitors again.

Dad said, 'Ooh, I loved being a

playground monitor.'

Grandpa said, '**IN MY DAY** we didn't have playgrounds. We had to sit on a patch of **CRACKED MUD** and be glad about it.'

And Mum said, 'I've just spent three hours listening to Mr Butterworth bang on about pencil sharpeners and the last thing I need is a heated debate about cracked mud. As long as Stanley's happy that's all that matters.'

And you know what, I am.

Because Mr Spigot rescued

Manjit's War of the Wizards wand and gave it a wash so it is definitely not **CONTAMINATED** any more.

And also because we all agreed that being playground monitor is a lot of responsibility and hard work and sometimes it's better just to play.

The
School Trip

Harvey Barlow says it's Manjit

Morris's fault for coming up with

a **FOOLPROOF PLAN** to rescue a

penguin in a rucksack.

Manjit says it's Lionel Dawes's

fault for saying the penguin

definitely looked sad and needed
rescuing in the first place when
in fact it just had a face that was
made like that.

And Lionel Dawes says it's
Mr Morris's fault for claiming he
could supervise us from behind
his newspaper instead of with
his actual eyes because he is an
UNDISCOVERED GENIUS.

Mr Nidgett says he doesn't
actually care whose fault it is
as long as the Penguin Madness
is over or he will LITERALLY

resign from
teaching and
become a
rocket scientist
because it
cannot be harder
than this.

I don't know whose fault it is,
but I do know it started with the
tadpole tank.

What happened was that 4A got
a bucket of frogspawn and a
tadpole tank so that they could

watch the **MIRACLE OF LIFE** in
front of their very eyes, because
the frogspawn would hatch into
tadpoles and the tadpoles would

turn into frogs and the frogs would be released into the wild, i.e. the newt pond behind the Smelly Death Log.

Harvey Barlow said what if
they actually hatched into
alligators?

Bruce Bingley said what if
Harvey Barlow actually hatched
into an alligator?

Manjit said he was going to
be the First Human Boy to Hatch
into an Alligator and he would eat
Bruce Bingley.

Lionel Dawes said they were
both **MAD** because frogspawn

definitely only hatches into frogs, or else it would be called alligatorspawn, and anyway it was unfair that we didn't get any frogspawn (because she is very keen on the **MIRACLE OF LIFE** and also releasing things into the wild).

Which is when Mr Nidgett agreed it was unfair but said it was also probably sensible because, as Mrs Bottomley-Blunt says, 4B's track record with animals is appalling, e.g.:

1. The time Bruce Bingley brought his real live rat Fingers in for Show and Tell and Fingers ran up Mrs Bottomley-Blunt's leg.

2. The time we went to the farm and a sheep got its head stuck between some railings because Harvey Barlow kept showing it his cheese sandwich.

3. The time we had a stick-insect tank and Lionel released them into the tree near the Poo Wagon and no one could find them again because of CAMOUFLAGE.

And in fact we were lucky we were even being allowed to go to Grimley Zoo tomorrow to draw all the animals or had we forgotten?

Immediately everyone was **MAD** with excitement because we **HAD** forgotten about the trip to Grimley Zoo and we had also forgotten that we were supposed to ask our parents if any of them could come with us for extra supervision, because Mrs Bottomley-Blunt says we need

constant monitoring and she does
not trust Mr Nidgett to be **UP TO
THE TASK**.

Manjit Morris said his mum could not come because she is too busy catching criminals because of being a policewoman.

Keith Mears said his mum could not come because she is too busy being the Queen.

Bruce Bingley said his mum could not come because of being the **OVERLORD OF THE UNIVERSE**, which Manjit said isn't even a thing.

 And Bruce said, 'Is.'

And Manjit said, 'Isn't.'

And Bruce said, 'Is.'

But Mr Nidgett said he didn't care if it was or wasn't a thing but could we please ask other less busy parents.

Which is when Lionel Dawes said her mum was less busy but she could not come because she does not believe in keeping animals in zoos, not even deadly bears or an endangered wasp, because it makes them **GLOOMY**, and in fact neither does Lionel so she would not come either.

But Mr Nidgett said in fact

zoos help protect deadly bears
and possibly even endangered
wasps so that they don't become
extinct, which means **LITERALLY**
dead forever, and if she doesn't
come then it is a day stocktaking
the stationery cupboard with
Mrs Pickens, who is the school
secretary and who smells of soup.

So Lionel said in fact she would
come, but would be checking for
any animals that looked even a
little bit gloomy, and releasing
them into the wild.

Mr Nidgett said actually she would probably not, because zoo security is very high, but that she could definitely **DRAW** a gloomy animal instead for a protest, because she is very keen on protests. Only if we didn't find any parents to come with us none of us would be drawing animals at all.

Bruce Bingley said that would be the end of the world.

Keith Mears said it would be the end of the universe.

But Mr Nidgett said it would not, it would just be the end of the trip and to please get on with naming all the capital cities in Europe, and not one of us got it right, not even Penelope Potts.

When I got home I asked Mum
and Dad and Grandpa if any of
them could come to the zoo.

But Dad said he had a crunch
meeting with the bigwigs so he
couldn't come.

Grandpa said he had a crunch
game of dominoes with Norman
Fazakerly so he couldn't come.

Mum said she had to listen
to Mr Butterworth bang on about
traffic cones so she couldn't
come.

And I was just saying that

actually this was
definitely the end
of the universe
when Manjit rang
and said his dad
was going to come
because he didn't

have a job because of being an

**UNDISCOVERED
GENIUS** and so
the universe was
LITERALLY
saved. And I
agreed.

So the next day we arrived
at school and so did Manjit's
dad, Mr Morris, and Muriel's
dad, Dr Lemon, who is against
most things because they are
MORTALLY DANGEROUS. And
almost immediately everyone
was **MAD** with excitement
because of going on a coach
again, because we have not been
allowed on a coach since the
time we went to the museum
on Mr Viceroy's rusty minibus

and Harvey Barlow drank four pink milks for a dare and was sick on the seat and the floor and the window and Mr Viceroy said never again.

Only it **WAS** again because then Mr Viceroy arrived, only not in the rusty minibus that smells of sick, but in a shiny new coach that had a vending machine for 'tasty snacks', another for 'hot and cold beverages', which means drinks, and a toilet with light-up buttons.

Except Dr Lemon said actually we would not be able to use any of them because taking off our seat belts would be **MORTALLY DANGEROUS** and Mr Nidgett agreed.

But no sooner were we off than Manjit said he needed a wee in a toilet with light-up buttons and if he didn't have one he would **LITERALLY** burst. And so he did.

And then Harvey Barlow said he needed a tasty snack and if he didn't get one he would **LITERALLY** faint. And so he did.

And then Keith Mears said
he was so cold his lips were
LITERALLY blue already (which
they were, but it was ink) and
if he didn't have a hot beverage
he would **LITERALLY** die of
hypothermia. And so he did. Only it
turned out his hot beverage, which
was beef soup, was only lukewarm
and so he wanted his money back.

 Only Mr Viceroy
said it was not.
And Keith said, 'Is.'
And Mr Viceroy said, 'Is not.'

And Mr Morris said he would
be the judge because he was an
UNDISCOVERED GENIUS and
he judged that it was definitely
lukewarm (and also mainly on Mr
Nidgett's shoes because we had
gone over a big bump, and so he had
to change into his emergency ones).

Which is when Dr Lemon said
distracting the driver with beef soup
was **MORTALLY DANGEROUS** and
to sit down with seat belts on and
sing 'Ten Green Bottles' until we got
to the zoo, only to start with 400

because it was quite a way away still.
And Muriel agreed. And so did Mr
Nidgett, so we did what Dr Lemon
said and we had only got to 347
green bottles when we arrived at
the zoo.

Then everyone was immediately
arguing about what animals we

should see first.

Lacey Braithwaite wanted to see the tigers.

Harvey Barlow wanted to see the giraffes.

Bruce Bingley wanted to see the dinosaurs, which Keith Mears said did not exist.

So Bruce Bingley said Keith Mears's brain did not exist.

And Keith Mears said Bruce Bingley's face did not exist.

Which is when Mr Nidgett said he was very close to wishing neither of them existed and to please get into our groups with our grown-up and to stick to them **LIKE GLUE** because they would be constantly monitoring us so that we were less likely to cause a **HOO-HA**, which is against Mrs Bottomley-Blunt's List of Rules.

So we did and our group was me and Manjit and Harvey and Mr Morris, who said he would definitely be constantly monitoring us for any **HOO-HA**, and Lionel, who said she would definitely be constantly monitoring the animals for any that looked a bit gloomy.

Then Mr Nidgett said whoever did the best drawing of an animal would get a prize. And Manjit said, 'Is it the joy of winning?', because that is not a real prize and everyone agreed.

But Mr Nidgett said it wasn't, it was a mug with a picture of a marmoset on it, which we agreed was definitely a real prize, and off we went.

First of all we went to see the capuchin monkeys, who were playing with a long piece of rope and a deflated rugby ball and a red sock.

Mr Morris said, 'Is that your sock, Manjit?'

Manjit said it was.

But Mr Morris said it definitely did not count as a **HOO-HA** because the monkeys were not gloomy and just to get on with drawing them while he read his paper.

I drew them like this.

Manjit drew them like this.

Lionel drew them like this.

Which Harvey said was made up and would be disqualified. And Mr Morris said he would be the judge and he judged: not disqualified.

Next we went to see the hippopotamuses, who were swimming in their tank with a model fox, which we said was **AMAZING** because we did not know hippos could swim.

Mr Morris said, 'Is that your model fox, Manjit?'

Manjit said it was.

But Mr Morris said it definitely did not count as a **HOO-HA** because the hippos were not gloomy and just to get on with drawing them while he read his paper.

I drew them
like this.

Manjit drew
them like this.

Lionel drew
them like this.

Which Harvey said was made up
too and would be disqualified.
And Mr Morris said he would
be the judge and he judged: not
disqualified. And he also judged
that it was time for lunch because
he was **WEARY** with all the
monitoring and needed a sandwich
to perk him up. So we all agreed,
but only if we could swap lunches,
because swapped lunches are the
BEST.

I ate Harvey's jam sandwiches
and an apple and a biscuit.

Manjit ate my cheese-and-apple sandwich and a tomato and a biscuit.

Harvey ate Manjit's chocolate-spread-and-hummus sandwiches and two bananas and a bag of crisps and half a watermelon and a tomato and an apple and five biscuits.

Lionel ate some seedy crackers and looked sad about it. Which is when Mr Morris said perhaps Lionel would like to swap for

one of his fish-finger-and-pickle
sandwiches, because he had eleven
spare. Only she said she would not
because:

1. They sounded disgusting.

2. She does not eat anything
with a face.

3. She was not sad about the
seedy crackers which were in
fact DELICIOUS and NUTRITIOUS,
but because none of the animals
looked gloomy and so she could not
draw sad animals for her protest
or release any into the wild.

So Manjit said after lunch we would definitely find a gloomy animal for her to draw. Mr Morris agreed and said he would monitor us closely from the shady bench possibly with his eyes shut because he is an **UNDISCOVERED GENIUS** and they can do things like that.

After lunch we went to see the flying foxes, but they didn't look gloomy.

Then we went to see the

horseshoe crabs, but they didn't look gloomy.

Then we went to see the ring-tailed lemurs and they definitely did not look gloomy.

Lionel said it was the worst trip ever and perhaps she would protest about that, so Manjit said we should go to see the penguins, because one of them definitely looked a bit gloomy when we went past earlier and it was a completely **FOOLPROOF PLAN**.

Manjit was right because

when we got to the penguin pool
most of the penguins were busy
whooshing in and out of the
water on a special slide except
for one who definitely did look
a bit gloomy, which Manjit said
was probably because of all the
others hogging the slide. And
Lionel said in fact we should
probably rescue it and release
it into the wild.

Manjit said in fact we could
release it at school, e.g. into the
newt pond.

But Lionel said it would eat the newts, which was **MURDER** because they had faces.

Only Manjit said it was not, it was the **CIRCLE OF LIFE** (because Lionel is keen on the **CIRCLE OF LIFE**) but today she wasn't so keen, which is when I said instead of the pond what about the broken slide instead? (Which is only half broken, because of the time Manjit put some glue on it.) It could have that slide all to itself, except at breaktime when the Year 3s use it

as gang headquarters. And everyone
agreed.

Lionel said, 'What about the
high security?'

Manjit said there wasn't any
because penguins do not bite and
also their fence is quite low because
of not being able to fly.

Harvey said, 'How do we fetch it?'

Manjit said he had another **FOOLPROOF PLAN** which is that Harvey could just lean over and lure the gloomy penguin into his empty rucksack using some leftover food as bait.

But Harvey said in fact he had eaten all his food, which was why his rucksack was empty. I had also eaten all my food.

Manjit had also eaten all his food.

Lionel had also eaten all her food even though it was only seedy biscuits.

Then Lionel was saying this
was the worst trip ever again when
I remembered that Mr Morris
still had eleven fish-finger-and-
pickle sandwiches left and fish
fingers were definitely something
penguins might like, and so we
could use those.

And so everyone agreed that
the **FOOLPROOF PLAN** would go
like this:

1. Harvey would dangle over the penguin fence while I held on to his feet.

2. Manjit would hand him a fish-finger-and-pickle sandwich to throw at the gloomy penguin.

3. Once the gloomy penguin had got a taste for the fish-finger-and-pickle sandwiches we would put one in the rucksack and the penguin would hop right in after it. Then it would be so full from all the sandwiches it would fall asleep until we got back on Mr Viceroy's coach which does not smell

of sick and back to school where
we could release it on to the slide
without ANY fuss or even HOO-HA.

And it almost worked.

What actually happened was that
the penguin **DID** eat the fish-finger
sandwich and did
not make one
bit of fuss or
HOO-HA when
it found out
there was
pickle in it.

It did not make one bit of fuss or **HOO-HA** when it got inside Harvey's rucksack and found another sandwich and also a seedy biscuit, which Lionel said would be nutritious for it and also encourage it to stop eating things with faces.

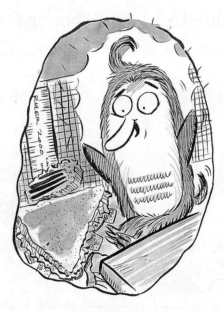

It did not make
one bit of fuss or
HOO-HA when we
woke up Mr Morris
by making a noise
like a howler monkey.

It did not make one bit of fuss
or **HOO-HA** when we got on Mr

Viceroy's coach
which does not
smell of sick and
started singing
'Four Hundred
Green Bottles'.

But that is when the **FOOLPROOF PLAN** went a little bit wrong.

Because when we got to 372 green bottles, the penguin started making a flapping sound.

I said it was because it was
afraid of the dark.

Lionel said it was because it
was feeling gloomy about eating
things with faces after all.

Harvey said it was because it was hungry and needed a snack. But I said we had run out of all our snacks and so Manjit said he would get one from the vending machine because he was a friend to the animals.

Then Harvey said he would get one because he was **BEST** friend to the animals.

But Lionel said she would get one because she was **QUEEN** of the animals.

Which is when Lacey Braithwaite peered over the top of the seat and said, 'Why are you causing a **HOO-HA**, which is against Mrs Bottomley-Blunt's rules, and also what are you doing with a penguin in a rucksack?'

Harvey said we did not have
a penguin in a rucksack.

Manjit said we did not have
a penguin in a rucksack.

Lionel said we did not have
a penguin in a rucksack.

I said we did not have a
penguin in a rucksack.

And it wasn't
even a lie, because
by that point the
penguin wasn't
in the rucksack
any more, it was
doing a poo on the
seat next to Muriel Lemon.

Then it did a
poo on the
seat next
to Bruce
Bingley.

Then it did a poo on Mr Nidgett's
Emergency Shoes, which is when
he told Mr Viceroy to stop the coach
because there had been a definite
HOO-HA.

Which is when Dr Lemon said,
'And also there is a deadly penguin
on board and it is **MORTALLY
DANGEROUS**.' And Muriel agreed.

Manjit said it was not, because
penguins do not have teeth.

But Dr Lemon said in fact we could catch bird flu, which can cause colds and coughs and also death.

Mr Nidgett said in fact coughs and colds and even death were the last thing we should be worrying about because why on earth did we have a penguin in the first place?

Which is when Harvey said it was Manjit's fault and Manjit said it was Lionel's fault and Lionel said it was Mr Morris's fault and Mr

Nidgett said he didn't care whose fault it was as long as the Penguin Madness was over or he would **LITERALLY** resign from teaching and become a rocket scientist because it could not be harder than this.

Which it was.

Because we went all the way back to the zoo and gave the penguin back to the zookeeper,

who pointed out that the penguin,
who was called Roy, was not in
any way gloomy, he just had a
face that was made like that.

Manjit said maybe Mrs
Bottomley-Blunt just has a face
that is made like that. And we
all agreed.

But she does not, because
when we got back to school, she
said we were the **WORST CLASS
IN THE WORLD** and that we
were also banned from school
trips **UNTIL KINGDOM COME**.

When I got home I told Mum and
Dad and Grandpa about the trip
to the zoo.

Dad said, 'I love a zoo.'

Grandpa said, 'In my day we didn't have zoos, we had **WOOLLY TIGERS** roaming the gardens and **SABRE-TOOTHED MAMMOTHS** in the shed and we were glad about it.'

And Mum said she had just spent two hours listening to Mr Butterworth bang on about zebra crossings and the last thing she needed was an argument about sabre-toothed anything and as long as Stanley was happy, that was all that mattered.

And do you know what? I am.

Because even though we aren't allowed back to the zoo or on the coach that does not smell of sick (but does smell of penguin poo), Mr Nidgett said my picture of a monkey chewing a sock was so excellent it definitely deserved the prize of a mug with a marmoset on it.

Mrs Bottomley-Blunt's List of Rules

1. No running in the corridors.

2. No sliding in the corridors.

3. No playing ludo in the corridors.

4. No outside voices inside.

5. No outside voices outside.

6. No putting paper in plugholes to see if it will block them.

7. No putting anything down the toilet.

8. Especially no putting PE kit down the toilet.

9. No eating in class.

10. No eating in the corridors.

11. No eating mud anywhere.

12. No claiming you will eat the class hamster.

13. No claiming you are secretly royal.

14. No claiming you are actually dead.

15. No claiming Major Wellington is a vampire.

16. No hats.

17. No badges.

18. No yo-yos.

19. No fake swords.

20. No real swords.

21. No wearing a colander on
    your head instead of a hat.

22. No being rude.

23. No being greedy.

24. No being too clever by half.

25. No War of the Wizards cards.

26. No War of the Wizards cloaks.

27. No War of the Wizards wands.

28. No ketchup.

Wizard hats are NOT uniform

29. No frogs in jars.

30. No frogspawn in jars

31. No claiming sago pudding is frogspawn.

32. No claiming bubble tea is frogspawn.

33. No claiming anything is frogspawn.

34. No pretending to be deaf.

35. No pretending to be daft.

Shopping

Rubbers
Soap
A loud bell
A mop
Ear plugs

36. No being daft.

37. No hitting each other.

38. No pinching each other.

39. No biting each other.

40. No poking each other.

41. No twisting anyone's ears.

42. No pulling anyone's hair.

43. No fighting in general.

44. No kerfuffle.

45. No shenanigans.

46. No tomfoolery.

47. No showing off.

48. No footling.

49. No fiddle-faddling.

50. No shilly-shallying.

Disappointing Day List
Keith Mears
Harvey Barlow
Bruce Bingley
All of 4B

Mrs Bottomley-Blunt's List of Rules Part 2

51. No eating a whole packet of biscuits.

52. No dropping one biscuit and then eating the rest of the packet.

53. No claiming a Ghost Pigeon ate half the packet.

54. No claiming a Ghost Pigeon ate your homework.

55. No claiming a Ghost Pigeon stole your PE kit.

56. No claiming a Ghost Pigeon spilt the paint.

57. No claiming Ghost Pigeons even exist.

58. No claiming Ghost Monkeys exist.

59. No claiming Ghost Teachers exist.

60. No claiming Major Wellington is a Ghost Teacher.

61. No fizzy drinks.

62. No fizzy sweets.

4B Zoo Trip
October 11th
(WARN ZOO)

63. No fireworks.

64. No pretend Nunchuks.

65. No actual Nunchuks.

66. No pushing anyone.

67. No prodding anyone.

68. No almost prodding anyone.

69. No stamping on things that have been dropped.

70. No stamping on other people's feet.

71. No stamping in general.

72. No flicking of ears.

73. No flicking of noses.

74. No flicking of rubbers across the room.

75. No flicking of pens on to the floor.

76. No flicking of peas at the dinner lady.

77. No flicking of sweetcorn at the dinner lady.

78. No flicking of anything ever.

79. No spilling soup and claiming it is ectoplasm.

80. No spilling custard and claiming it is ectoplasm.

81. No spilling pink milk and claiming it is ectoplasm.

82. No claiming anything is ectoplasm.

83. No pink milk.

84. No brown milk.

85. No milk except milk milk.

86. No going to the toilet without permission.

87. No going to the toilet to discuss War of the Wizards.

88. No going to the toilet to play Wrestling Club.

89. No going to the toilet unless you actually need the toilet.

90. No Wrestling Club.

New girl
Bridget Pickersgill
Class 4B?

91. No War of the Wizards Club.

92. No Vampire Club.

93. No Thinking Up New Clubs Club.

94. No singing the wrong words to hymns.

95. No burping hymns.

96. No burping at all in assembly.

97. No trying to hold your breath for ten minutes in assembly.

98. No trying to make anyone else hold their breath for ten minutes in assembly.

99. No doing anything in assembly except listening and being NEAT and OBEDIENT.

100. No cats.

N.U.T.

Mrs. Bottomley-Blunt
Head Teacher
ID#AUG2ND1979

Could you be in

THE

WORST

CLASS

IN THE

WORLD?

Turn over and take
a fun quiz to find out!

1. If someone gave you a jam sandwich to flush down the toilet, would you do it?
YES or NO

2. Have you ever flushed something down the toilet that you shouldn't?
YES or NO

3. If your answer to number 2 was YES, did the toilet then flood the bathroom?
YES or NO

4. Have you ever eaten a fish-finger-and-pickle sandwich?
YES or NO

5. Would you feed a penguin a fish-finger-and-pickle sandwich?
YES or NO

6. Would you hide a penguin in your rucksack?
YES or NO

ANSWERS

Mostly YES — You could absolutely be one of the Worst Class in the World! Come and join in the fun!

Mostly NO — Sorry, you're probably more suited to being in Class 4A, but you can definitely still play with 4B at breaktime!

Have you read
the madness and mayhem
in

THE

WORST

CLASS

IN THE

WORLD

OUT NOW!

Read on for a sneak peek...

(Shh! Don't tell Mrs Bottomley-
Blunt we showed you!)

Lacey Braithwaite says it's Harvey Barlow's fault for bringing in discount biscuits.

Harvey Barlow says it's Manjit Morris's fault for offering him a broken yo-yo and a stone that might be a dinosaur claw for a discount biscuit.

Manjit says it's Lacey Braithwaite's fault for claiming her biscuits are superior, and also for being so mean with her biscuits in the first place.

Mr Nidgett says he doesn't actually care whose fault it is as long as the Biscuit Madness is finished or he will **LITERALLY** resign from teaching and become a llama farmer because it cannot be harder than this.

I don't know whose fault it is, but I do know it started on Monday.

What happened was that Manjit and me were footling around at first break, up to nothing in particular, when Manjit saw Lacey Braithwaite hiding behind the Smelly Death Log, i.e. the hollow log with the bird poo on it, which no one even goes near unless they are up to **NO GOOD**. Not since Bruce Bingley claimed it had an ancient curse on it and if you touched the poo for more than a second you would be swallowed by The Ghost Pigeon.

Manjit said we should spy on Lacey and see what she was up to, because it was bound to be **SUSPICIOUS**. Which it totally was.

Joanna Nadin is an award-winning author who has written more than eighty books for children. She has also been a juggler, a lifeguard and an adviser to the Prime Minister. The worst thing she ever did at school was be sick on her plate at lunch and blame it on someone else. She lives in Bath and her favourite things are goats, monkeys and crisps.

Rikin Parekh (aka Mr Rik) is an author/illustrator and ninja. He also works in primary schools as an LSA and worked as a bookseller (which was REALLY, REALLY fun!). The worst thing he ever did at school was to draw all over his exercise books (and in the margins!) and then get a big telling off for it! He lives in Wembley and his favourite things are pizza, dogs, and picking his nose and collecting the bogeys.

LOOK OUT FOR MORE
HILARIOUS HIGH JINKS WHEN

THE

WORST

CLASS

IN THE

WORLD

DARES YOU!

COMING SOON!